For Asha – my inspiration
– *E.L*

For Jan and Luke
– *B.B*

First American edition published 1993 by
Crocodile Books, USA
An imprint of Interlink Publishing Group, Inc.
99 Seventh Avenue, Brooklyn, New York 11215
First published in 1992 by Magi Publications,
London, Great Britain

Library of Congress Cataloging-in-Publication Data available
LC 92-33326
Printed and bound in Italy
ISBN 1–56656–118–3

· Jamie & Luke ·
Asleep at Last

· Ewa Lipniacka · Basia Bogdanowicz ·

Crocodile Books, USA

An imprint of Interlink Publishing Group, Inc.
NEW YORK

"Bedtime!" said Mom and Dad.
The family had been shopping all day, and everyone was tired.

"Tonight it's Daddy's turn to take you up to bed,"
called Mom. "I'm going to put the shopping away."

"A quick face wash will have to do," said Dad, "or you'll both be asleep on your feet."

Jamie gathered all the toys he couldn't bear to go to sleep without.

Daddy made Luke take off his boots, even though
they were brand new.

And he wouldn't let Jamie sleep in his shiny new raincoat, either.

To be fair, he also took off Oscar's new collar and put it away until tomorrow.

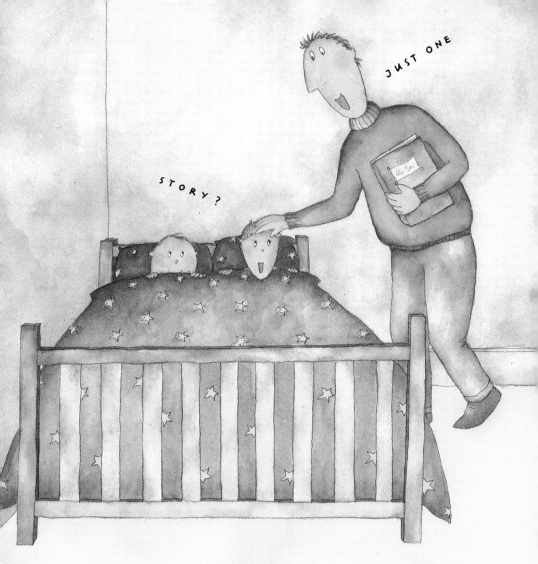

Then he tucked the boys into bed . . .

. . . and began reading a story.

After a while, Mom said to herself, "Why is Daddy taking such a long time? The boys were so tired when they went upstairs."

"Are they asleep yet?" she called up the stairs.

Then a small voice that sounded a lot like Luke's answered, "Yes, they're both asleep!"